Farmer Girl

By Deborah Ann Martin

Burning Bulb
PUBLISHING

Farmer Girl

By Deborah Ann Martin

Farmer Girl
by Deborah Ann Martin

Burning Bulb Publishing
P.O. Box 4721
Bridgeport, WV 26330-4721
United States of America

www.burningbulbpublishing.com

Book design and illustrations by Héctor J. Valdez
hola@hecjvaldez.com

First Edition

ISBN 978-1-948278-55-3

Printed in the United States of America

Happiness doesn't come
from what you have.

There was once a sad prince
handsome and fair.

He wanted a bride who really cared.

He told his father his plan to
be hungry and poor.

Throughout the kingdom, he
would explore.

He dressed as a beggar with clothes ragged and torn, covered in dirt, and shoes broken and worn.

When he knocked on a Duke's door, it jerked open knocking him to the floor.

His daughter saw the beggar dirty and weak. She let out and awful shriek!

She did not want his kind near her door. So, she had guards remove the beggar, hungry and poor.

At each house, he was rejected and turned away.

As night fell, a tired prince
returned home to lay.

On an old farm lived an orphan
girl who cared. She loved
people and always shared.

Deep inside, she had a heart of gold. She worked hard on the farm in the heat or cold.

Each day she tended the chickens and sheep. In the fields, she planted vegetables and wheat.

Even though she didn't have a cent, she was happy and content.

Months went by with no hope in sight. Hopeless and tired, the prince saw a farmhouse in the distant light.

He knocked on the door to find no one home. He looked in the fields and saw the farmer girl alone.

He stumbled to the fields and
fell at her feet. He begged and
pleaded for something to eat.

The girl's heart filled with sadness
cried a single tear. She took his hand
and explained that she lived near.

She cooked her best meal and a cake with fruit. After they ate, she played on her flute.

They talked the night away. Then, she
asked the beggar to stay.

Unlike the others, she had beauty within. That day, the prince's heart she did win.

The prince asked her to be his wife.
She agreed to be together for the rest
of their lives.

The prince told her how happy he did
feel. Tomorrow he had a secret he
would reveal.

He had to leave her for just one night. He assured her everything would be alright.

When he returned to tell the king, he
was given the royal wedding ring.

Preparations were made for the wedding
and feast. He invited the entire kingdom
and the priest.

The king sent the royal carriage
to pick up the bride for the
prince's marriage.

Attending the wedding wasn't part of
her plan until the invitation was placed
in her hand.

She had no beautiful gown to be worn.
All she had was a dress slightly torn.

At the castle, she didn't understand, why so many wanted to give her a hand.

The maidens wanted to fix her hair. The confused farmer girl asked why she was there.

They showed her the corner with her wedding gown. In disbelief, her happy face turned to a frown.

She did not want to marry the Prince
today. She had fallen in love with the
beggar yesterday.

She felt forced to walk down the aisle.
Forgetting the beggar would be denial.

When the priest asked if she agreed to
marry, her answer was "no."

She Replied, "I can marry for love alone. I want to go home."

She started to run away when the prince
took her hand and asked her to stay.

He said, "Last night I told you how I feel.
Being a Prince is the secret I had to reveal.

You gave your best when I was fed. I fell in
love and asked you to wed."

The other women who turned the
beggar away now wished they had asked
him to stay.

After the wedding that no one would
forget, The Royal Couple happily rode
off into the sunset.

Farmer Girl

Made in United States
Orlando, FL
02 March 2023